Fields of F...

EGMONT
We bring stories to life

First published in Great Britain 2008
by Egmont UK Limited, 239 Kensington High Street, London W8 6SA
© 2008 Prism Art & Design Limited, a HIT Entertainment company.
Based on an original idea by D. Gingell, D. Jones and characters created by R. M. J. Lee.
The Fireman Sam name and character are trademarks of Prism Art & Design Limited,
a HIT Entertainment company.

ISBN 978 1 4052 3813 7
1 3 5 7 9 10 8 6 4 2
Printed in Singapore

One sunny day, Fireman Sam was blowing up an inflatable dam outside Pontypandy Fire Station when Trevor Evans came along.

"What have you got there, Sam?" asked Trevor. "A blow-up birthday cake?!"

"No, Trevor," smiled Sam. "This is what we use to store water when we're fighting a fire and there's no tap nearby."

"I'd love to see it in action," replied Trevor. "But I'm taking Mandy and Norman to the seaside." And Trevor jumped into his bus and waved goodbye.

As Trevor drove off, the bus exhaust made a loud bang.

"Mmm, that doesn't sound too healthy . . ." said Sam.

The bus continued to make loud bangs as Trevor drove through the countryside.

"Did you just sit on a balloon, Mr Evans?" giggled Norman.

"Very funny, Norman," replied Trevor. "But it won't be so funny if the bus breaks down."

"I hope it breaks down when we get to the seaside!" said Mandy.

Then the bus made three loud bangs, and little puffs of smoke came out of the exhaust, before it stopped.

Trevor got off the bus and looked under the bonnet. He told Norman, Mandy and Dusty to get out and stretch their legs.

"But Mr Evans, I want to go to the seaside!" said Norman.

"We won't be going anywhere unless I can fix this!" replied Trevor. "You wait there and don't wander off."

Norman and Mandy looked at a funny sign near the gate, but just when they had worked out that it meant 'no campfires', they realised Dusty had disappeared.

"Come on, let's go find him," said Norman.

At the Fire Station, Station Officer Steele, Sam and Elvis were standing around the dam. Tom Thomas' helicopter was hovering high up above with a large plastic bucket filled with water.

"Sam to Wallaby One. Lower away!" said Sam into his walkie-talkie.

"OK, mate," replied Tom, carefully lowering the bucket.

But as Elvis tried to catch it, he tipped the water over Station Officer Steele.

"Sorry, Sir!" blushed Elvis.

In the countryside, Dusty was barking loudly as he chased a fieldmouse. Norman and Mandy were close behind.

"Look! Someone hasn't put their campfire out," said Mandy, as she spotted a smoking fire on the ground. "We should tell Trevor."

"OK, but let's find Dusty first," said Norman. "Come back, Dusty!"

And Norman and Mandy chased off after Dusty, just as the campfire set alight again!

Meanwhile, Trevor was busy fiddling under the bonnet of the bus.

"There we are, kids! I think that will fix it!" he said, closing the bonnet. But then Trevor realised that Norman and Mandy had gone.

"Mandy! Norman! Come back at once!" he shouted, turning to the fields.

Norman and Mandy were still chasing after Dusty. They had just realised that he was trying to catch a fieldmouse, when it escaped into a hole in a tree trunk. Dusty, Mandy and Norman stopped suddenly and landed in a heap on the ground.

"It's gone really foggy," said Norman, as smoke billowed across them.

"That's not fog, Norman, it's smoke!" said Mandy. "It must be that campfire!"

"Mr Evans! Help! We can't see where we're going!" Norman and Mandy shouted.

On the roadside, Trevor could faintly hear Norman and Mandy calling out in the distance. He looked over the wall and saw some smoke rising from the field.

"Oh my goodness!" cried Trevor. He got out his mobile phone and dialled 999.

"Which service do you require?" asked the operator on the other end of the line.

At Pontypandy Fire Station, Station Officer Steele picked up the emergency message. "Action Stations, everyone! A field is burning on the coast road, and Norman and Mandy are stuck in it!" he said.

"There's no water for miles around there!" said Fireman Sam. "Elvis, you load the dam and I'll radio Tom." And he made the call to Mountain Rescue.

Quick as a flash, Jupiter was heading out of the Fire Station, with Sam, Elvis and Station Officer Steele in the cab.
Nee Nah! Nee Nah!

Meanwhile, Tom Thomas flew off in his rescue helicopter.

The field was now thick with smoke.

"Norman! Where are you?" coughed Mandy.

"Let's hold hands, so we don't lose each other!" said Norman, feeling scared.

"And I'll hold on to Dusty's collar," said Mandy.

Then they heard Jupiter's siren. "That sounds like Sam! Help! Help!" shouted Norman and Mandy.

Jupiter raced along the country lanes with her blue lights flashing and stopped next to Trevor and the bus. Sam, Elvis and Station Officer Steele leapt out and headed across the field with the hoses and the dam. By now the field was filled with smoke.

"Help! Help! We're over here!" shouted Norman.

"Trevor, help Elvis with the dam. I'm going to radio Tom!" said Sam.

Tom was flying over Pontypandy Lake. The helicopter swooped down and the huge bucket splashed into the water, filling up to the brim.

"I'm picking up the water now! Be with you in two minutes, Sam!" said Tom into his headset.

Then he set off towards the field with the bucket of water juddering beneath.

The dam was now set up. Sam and Elvis strapped on their breathing apparatus.

"Right, men. I'll supervise the water drop," said Officer Steele. "Sam, find those children!" And Sam and Elvis took the hoses and walked into the smoke.

In the sky above, the helicopter lowered the bucket towards the inflatable dam.

"Right a bit. That's it!" said Officer Steele, tipping the water into the dam. "That's it, Tom. Take her away."

And Wallaby One flew off.

Sam and Elvis set their hoses on the fire and soon the smoke started to billow away. Dusty raced towards them and Norman and Mandy trooped sadly alongside.

"Thank goodness you're alright!" said Sam. "You gave us quite a fright wandering off like that."

"Sorry, Sam. You can let go now, Mandy," said Norman, looking at his hand.

"You mean you can!" replied Mandy. "It wasn't me that wanted to hold hands!"

It was now too late for Trevor to take Mandy and Norman to the seaside, but Sam told him to bring them to the Fire Station instead. When they arrived, it looked like a mini seaside, with a palm tree and sand next to the dam!

"Wow! Sam, this is great!" said Mandy and Norman.

"We just need to top up the dam, so you can have a dip," said Sam. And Tom's helicopter flew overhead.

"I've got it, Sir!" said Elvis. But he tipped the bucket of water over Station Officer Steele again!

Norman and Mandy tried their best to hide their giggles!

Stay Safe!

Can you remember what to do if a fire breaks out?

Get out.
Get the Fire Brigade out.
Stay out!

Sam's Safety Tips

 Never play with matches or lighters.

 If you smell smoke or see fire, tell a grown-up.

 Don't play near hot ovens, or boiling pots and pans.

 Keep toys and clothes away from fires and heaters.

Ask a grown-up to fit a smoke alarm in your house and test it regularly.

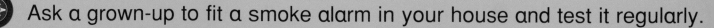